BEACH DAY

By Fran Manushkin
Illustrated by Kathy Wilburn

Dedicated to 12th Street Beach

A GOLDEN BOOK · NEW YORK

Western Publishing Company, Inc., Racine, Wisconsin 53404

"Good morning," Daddy says. I open my eyes, and the sun shines in. Daddy's face is sunny, too, and warm when I hug him. "Remember? Today's beach day," he says.

"Hurray!" I shout.

I'm in my suit, and Daddy's still washing the car. WHOOSH!—he shoots the hose at me. I run away, so he shoots water up to the trees. It makes the leaves shiny white.

"Want a drink?" he asks.

"Oh, yes!" And he swooshes a stream at me.

Mama says, "Everybody in the car!" I sit on a towel because I'm wet. The car goes slow, then faster and faster. WHEEEE!—there goes my hair out the window.

Mama turns on the radio, and we all sing along LOUD. Then we make a big turn, and we're at the beach.

Guess who's in the water first! The waves are co-o-o-old and taste salty, and the sun is so hot, it makes me see dots.

All at once a whale comes and grabs my foot. "It's Daddy!" I scream, and Mama saves me.

Then Mama splashes me up and down. We try to bounce
Daddy, but he's too big. So we shake our hair all over him
like dogs.

Then, by myself, I do blindman's float—with my eyes open. When I come up, I see rainbows around Mama and Daddy.

All of us float to the sand, then. Daddy buries me so I'll dry fast. Then Mama and I bury him. It takes a lot of sand.

We get hungry, and Daddy has to go for ice cream. Mine is lemon-fizz, wrapped in a napkin.

"Let's go for a walk, little mermaid," Daddy says.

He goes first, and I try to fill up his steps before the sea does.

Daddy races the waves and wins! He's faster than the sea.

We get seashells, too. Mine are gold and yellow, and shiny like the sea. I put them in a plastic bag with water so they'll stay sunny forever.

Daddy gets white shells like the gas-station sign, and he jingles them in his pocket.

I show Mama mine when we get back, and Daddy gives her his and bows.
   She laughs!

After a while, Daddy says, "Well, I think it's time to go."
I cry, but he says we'll come back soon.

Our car is hot, so we go fast to make a breeze.
Then the sun gets golden. It slides down the sky while we race it faster and faster through the trees.

Everything around us is glowing. We're going over a bridge, and the water is gold, and the sailboats are floating—gold, too.

It's cool now, so Mama puts a sweater on me. I'm getting sleepy, so Mama sings,

> "Hush-a-bye, don't you cry.
> Go to sleepy, little baby.
> When you wake, you'll have cake
> And all the pretty little horses."

Lights are blinking on in houses.

Bumpy-bump, I feel with my eyes closed. One more bump and we're home.

I pretend I'm sleeping so Daddy can carry me upstairs. He steers me to bed. "Give me a glass of water," I tell him.

"Haven't you swallowed enough today?" he says. But he brings it.

Then he whispers, "Good night, golden mermaid."
"Glub-glub!" I whisper and hug him tight.

Then I close my eyes, still tasting the sea, and rocking on the waves, and floating to sleep in the night.